For my Mom, Donna.
And for Spencer
— Cori

For Dad,
Who saw the world differently
— Sinead

THE BEST YOU CAN BE

Cori Brooke

Art by Sinead Hanley

FIVE MILE

Sometimes you may feel
you can't do all of the things.

And everywhere you look
you see great queens and kings.

But look closer at yourself and your abilities.

You'll see in your talents a world of possibilities.

What can you do?
Add it all up.

What you will have
is a very full cup.

So you may never come first in a running race.

Instead you dance with elegance and grace.

Maybe you'd rather not
be the school leader.

That's okay, you might be
a super-fast reader.

You might never win
a single school prize or award.

But you're brave and always
first off the high diving board.

We aren't all the same, and that's a good thing.
We're all meant to sound unique when we sing.

If you try and don't give up
you will get another turn.

And if you try your hardest,
you'll get better as you learn!

You might never be the
top of your grade,

but you look after others
with your first aid.

You might be happiest
doing a good deed,

and offering kindness
to people in need.

Perhaps you stayed to help,
when everyone else ran?

Maybe you give the best cuddles
when no-one else can.

It's okay if your talents
aren't showy or loud,

for your special gifts,
you should be very proud.

$$2x + y = 2$$
$$8^3 = 8 \times 8 \times 8$$

A
C
B

You might never be able
to do a cool trick,

but you might love numbers
and arithmetic.

You might never be
a wonderful cook.

But maybe one day you'll
write a best-selling book.

You might spend your weekends
making sure others are fed,

or maybe you're great at
thinking many moves ahead.

Your brain might see things
in a way that's new and unique.

Embrace your passions,
release your inner geek.

Or have fun doing things
you aren't very good at.

Dance like no-one's watching.
Wear the craziest hat.

At times you may feel
you can't do all of the things.

You still can fly high
because you have your own wings.

Just embrace everything
about you that's brilliant,

And you'll shine like the stars
and be so resilient.

You're right on your way when you know and believe
that doing your best is the best you can be.

To have fun trying makes you a king or queen.
So wear your crown proudly. Let it be seen.

Made with love by the team at

FIVE MILE

Rocco, Graham, Bridget, Kate & Victoria

Five Mile, the publishing division of Regency Media

www.fivemile.com.au

First published 2022.
This paperback edition published 2023.

Written by Cori Brooke
Text copyright © Cori Brooke, 2023
Illustrations by Sinead Hanley
Illustrations copyright © Sinead Hanley, 2023

ISBN: 978 1 92294 330 9

Printed in China   5 4 3 2 1

A catalogue record for this
book is available from the
National Library of Australia

This page is stuck down